The
GOOSE *Who*
Wrote a BOOK

The GOOSE Who Wrote a BOOK

by Judy Delton

illustrations by Catherine Cleary

Carolrhoda Books, Inc. / Minneapolis

for Susan Pearson

LIBRARY OF CONGRESS CATALOGING IN PUBLICATION DATA

Delton, Judy.
The goose who wrote a book.

(A Carolrhoda on my own book)
Summary: When Goose, upon the advice of her
friends, changes the main character in her
story, the publisher stipulates that the
character should be the original absent-minded
bear.
[1. Authorship—Fiction. 2. Geese—Fiction]
I. Cleary, Catherine, ill. II. Title.
PZ7.D388Go   [E]   81-15475
ISBN 0-87614-179-3   AACR2

1 2 3 4 5 6 7 8 9 10 00 99 98 97 96 95 94 93 92 91

Once there was a goose
who wanted to be a writer.
Everyone said, "Silly Goose!
You can't be a writer.
How many geese do you know
who write books?
None!"

But Goose was a die-hard.

Day after day she wrote.

Short stories about

the education of baby goslings.

Middle-sized stories about

the habits of homing pigeons.

Poems about Japanese song birds.

But the best thing she ever wrote

was a long story about

an absent-minded bear.

She was so pleased with it

that she ran right to Bear's house

and showed it to him.

"What do you think?" she said,
tapping her wings
on his kitchen table.
She was not a patient goose.
Bear was not a fast reader.
It took him some time

to read the whole thing.
By the time he finished,
Goose was pulling out
her tail feathers.
"Well?" she said.
"Let's have it."

Bear took off his glasses.

He put them on top

of his refrigerator.

"It's silly," he said.

"Bears are not absent-minded."

"Of course not," said Goose.

"This is FICTION.

It's not TRUE, Bear.

It's just a story."

"Just the same," said Bear.

"Professors are absent-minded.

Bears are not.

You should change the bear

to a professor, Goose."

11

"Cheese Louise," said Goose,

feeling low.

Bear handed the story back to her.

"I could have read it better

if I'd had my glasses on," he said.

"You did have your glasses on, Bear."

"Why, no.

My glasses are . . ."

"On top of the refrigerator,"
said Goose.

"You just put them there."

"I don't remember that," said Bear.

Goose handed him his glasses.

"Change the bear, Goose.

To a...a..."

"A professor, Bear.

You told me to change him

to a professor."

"That's not a bad idea," said Bear.

He looked surprised.

Goose went home.

She wrote the story over.

She changed the bear to a professor.

It took her 4 hours and 12 minutes.

Then she put her pencil behind her ear

and went to see the professor.

"I just wrote a new story.

Do you have time to read it?"

The professor looked for his glasses.

He looked on top of the book case.

He looked under his pipe rack.

He looked in his desk drawer.

He looked in his vest pocket.

"Professor," said Goose.

"I don't believe you wear glasses.

You have 20/20 vision.

Read it just with your eyes."

The professor snapped his fingers.

"I believe you are right," he said.

The professor read Goose's story.

Then he read it again.

Goose paced the floor.

She twirled her pencil.

She took a run around
the professor's house.

She took a swim in his lily pond.
She hated to wait.
Waiting seemed to be
the story of her life.

"So let's have it, Professor,"
she said.
"Isn't it great?
Shall I autograph one of
my tail feathers for you?"
The professor frowned.
"I don't think the hero
should be a professor," he said.
"Cheese Louise," said Goose.
She bit her pencil in half.
"Bear thought a professor
would be just right."
The professor shook his head.
"Feels wrong," he said.
"Professors are not absent-minded."

He scratched his head.

Then he forgot and scratched it again.

"I have it!" he said.

"Change the professor

to a second-grade teacher.

Second-grade teachers

are popular today.

And they are certainly absent-minded.

Why, I just read about

a second-grade teacher

who was so absent-minded

that she forgot to dry her laundry.

She put the sheets on her bed

soaking wet!"

Goose looked at the professor.

His shirt sleeves were wet.

"Cheese Louise!" she said.

"I'm sick of writing this thing over."

"But I'm certain it needs
a second-grade teacher,"
said the professor.

Goose grabbed her story
and left angrily.
She kicked leaves and cans
and popsicle sticks
all the way home.

When she got home, she sat down.

Maybe he is right, she thought.

He is a professor, after all.

So she wrote the story over again.

She made the professor

a second-grade teacher.

It took her 6 hours and 14 minutes.

When she finished,

she had wing cramp.

"This is the last time," she said.

"I am not showing this story

to another friend.

No one will see it

until it is a book."

Goose typed the new story carefully.

Then she put it in an envelope.

She put a stamp on it.

She wrote RUSH in red letters

on the back.

She wrote the name

of the book company

on the front.

Then she mailed it.

Goose came home.

She pulled down her shades.

She lay down on her bed.

"Cheese Louise," she said.

"I'm tired.

Being a writer is hard work."

She closed her eyes

and fell asleep for 11 hours.

When she woke up,
she was very hungry.
She fixed egg foo young
and fried rice.

"Now all I can do
is wait to hear
from the book company,"
she said.
"I hate waiting!"

Every morning
Goose met the postman at the door.
Every morning
the postman handed her an envelope
that was not from the book company.
On Monday he handed her a card.
It said,

Give blood for sick geese.

4:00 PM   Tuesday
City Hall

On Tuesday he handed her a letter. It said,

Dear Goose:
Lucky you!
You and your family
can now get six weeks
of *Goose Digest*
for only $3.86!

On Wednesday he handed Goose
her copy of *Tame* magazine.

But on Thursday he handed her
a large white envelope.
It was from the book company.

Panda
Pub. Co.

Dear Goose,

We will make your story into a book.
But the hero should be
an absent-minded bear
instead of a second-grade teacher.

"Cheese Louise," said Goose.
She took her first story
about the absent-minded bear
out of her desk drawer.

"I always did like this story best,"
she said.

Then she took out her red pen.
She turned to the last page
of her story.
In big red letters
at the bottom of the page
she wrote: